Cursed Crusaders

by Penumbra Quill

Little, Brown and Company
New York Boston

Little, Brown and Company
Hachette Book Group
1290 Avenue of the Americas, New York, NY 10104
Visit us at LBYR.com
mylittlepony.com

First Edition: April 2018

Little, Brown and Company is a division of Hachette Book Group, Inc. The Little, Brown name and logo are trademarks of Hachette Book Group, Inc.

The publisher is not responsible for websites (or their content) that are not owned by the publisher.

Library of Congress Control Number 2017959123

ISBNs: 978-0-316-47571-6 (pbk.), 978-0-316-47572-3 (ebook)

Printed in the United States of America

LSC-C

10 9 8 7 6 5 4 3 2 1

Rarity, Applejack, and Rainbow Dash stood glaring at the Schoolhouse. Snips, Snails, Twist, Pip, and every other young pony had rushed down the steps, excited that school was done for the day. But the three fillies *they* were waiting for had apparently vanished without a trace. Despite being grounded, Sweetie Belle, Apple Bloom, and Scootaloo had broken strict instructions to stay put and were now Celestia-knew-where.

"I simply can*not* believe this," Rarity muttered.

"We shoulda seen it coming." Rainbow Dash shrugged. "We woulda done the same thing." She and Rarity both turned to look at Applejack, who seemed as if she was fit to be tied.

"Y'all thought it was bad when Celestia banished Luna to the moon?" she growled. "Just wait till ya see what I do to my little sister."

CHAPTER ONE

The Everfree Forest was big. Scootaloo *knew* that, but she'd never really appreciated *how* big until she spent an entire night walking in it. She squinted in the dim light of sunrise, trying to see beyond the trees ahead. They had to be close to Ponyville by now...right?

Then again, the sooner they were back in Ponyville, the sooner she'd have to face Rainbow Dash, Aunt Holiday, and Auntie Lofty. And they would *not* be happy with Scootaloo for sneaking out of school without telling anypony. She racked her brain for a way to explain: *Funny story, but Princess Luna appeared to us in our dreams and said we were destined to protect the Livewood from anypony trying to steal the Helm of Shadows*...Nah. The only thing funny about that was how crazy it sounded. Not for the first time, Scootaloo wondered if Luna had made a mistake. It had happened before. . . .

"Hold up, y'all," called Apple Bloom.

"What's wrong?" Sweetie Belle asked, looking around nervously. Scootaloo couldn't blame her. After meeting a peryton, being stalked by Timberwolves, and getting bespelled by Auntie Eclipse in the same night, they were all a little on edge.

"We need a plan," Apple Bloom said. "Which is why I'm callin' a special meetin' of the Cutie Mark Crusaders to order!" She banged her hoof against a nearby rock and gestured to a hastily made agenda, constructed out of sap-covered leaves stuck on a tree trunk.

Scootaloo shared a smile with Sweetie Belle as they walked over to join their friend. Apple Bloom could hold a meeting anywhere.

"First item of business…" Apple Bloom continued. "We're Defenders of the Livewood now! That's a big responsibility. We gotta be prepared for Auntie Eclipse's next attack."

"Shouldn't we just tell Princess Twilight Sparkle what happened and leave it to her?" Scootaloo asked. She didn't like thinking it was up to them alone to protect Equestria from the creation of another Nightmare Moon. That was the kind of thing you couldn't mess up. *And when it comes to messing up*, Scootaloo thought, *the Cutie Mark Crusaders don't have the best track record.*

"Princess Luna said our matching cutie marks mean we're the only ponies who can keep the Livewood safe," Sweetie Belle reminded Scootaloo. "We'll definitely need help from our sisters and their friends, but this is up to us."

"And Applejack will finally see that we're

just as brave and ready for adventure as they are!" Apple Bloom grinned.

Scootaloo wasn't sure her friends had thought through this all. Keeping the Helm of Shadows away from three powerful Unicorns was going to be dangerous, if not impossible. So she skipped ahead to the next thing on the agenda.

"Lubby Mom and Amble Mrrr?" asked Scootaloo, squinting as she tried to read Apple Bloom's leaf chart.

"Lilymoon and Ambermoon," Apple Bloom translated, then shrugged. "It's kinda hard to write usin' tree sap."

"I hope they're okay," Sweetie Belle said with concern.

"Me too," Scootaloo agreed. She was worried about her friends. The Moon sisters' family had always creeped her out, but now that she knew Blue Moon, Lumi Nation, and Auntie Eclipse were using dark magic, that was another whole level of scary. The Crusaders had to find some way to warn Ambermoon and Lilymoon about their dangerous relatives. It was obvious the two sisters had no idea what their family was up to, but Scootaloo wasn't convinced that would protect them from Auntie Eclipse.

"We'll make sure Twilight knows that Ambermoon and Lilymoon are on our side," Apple Bloom said. "She'll be able to keep 'em safe, no matter what their family tries! Now, agenda item number three—"

But Scootaloo never found out what three was. Because just then, she heard the spooky croak of Auntie Eclipse's laugh.

CHAPTER TWO

In a panic, Scootaloo threw her hooves around Sweetie Belle and Apple Bloom and flapped her wings with all her might. With a fluttering tumble, the three fillies bounced to a stop behind a large fern. They huddled, hiding, as familiar voices filtered through the nearby trees.

"Auntie, don't laugh. I really think we're going the wrong way," Lilymoon protested, stepping into the clearing where the Crusaders had been moments before.

"I already told you. You're going exactly where you need to," Auntie said, her voice suddenly sharp.

"But the house is that way," Ambermoon said, frowning and pointing a hoof in the opposite direction.

"So it is," Auntie purred, "but we won't be going back to the house. Today we're taking a nice long walk. I want you fillies to help me with a little magical project. You'd do that for your dear auntie, right?"

Peering out from behind the fern, Scootaloo watched in horror as Auntie's horn began to glow. "She's going to cast a spell on them! We have to stop her!" Scootaloo whispered fiercely. She was about to leap out from behind the fern, but her friends held her back.

"She wouldn't hurt her own nieces, would she?" Sweetie Belle gasped, eyes wide.

"Look, it's just a beacon spell," Apple Bloom whispered in relief. Sure enough, Auntie had sent a pulse of blue magic out through the trees.

"So? We still have to rescue them! They're our friends. Who knows what that crazy pony has planned?" Scootaloo demanded under her breath.

"We need to follow them to find out," Apple Bloom argued quietly, "so we can tell Twilight! If we blow our cover now, we'll never know!"

"What do you think, Sweetie Belle?" Scootaloo whispered. But she saw that the young Unicorn had a strange look on her face. "Uh...Sweetie Belle?"

"Sorry," Sweetie Belle said, "I was just thinking—isn't a beacon spell used to show somepony where you are?"

"And it worked," a weirdly cheerful voice sang out from behind Scootaloo. She jumped, spinning to see a grinning Blue Moon walking up behind them. Lumi Nation followed a hoofbeat behind. When she spotted the Crusaders, she snarled.

"You again?"

"Run!" yelled Scootaloo. The trio burst from their hiding spot, racing into the cover of the trees. Hoofbeats thundered after them. Scootaloo put her head down and galloped as fast as she could. If the Moon family caught them now, she thought, they'd never be able to warn Twilight or guard the Helm of Shadows or protect Equestria. Luna *really* should've picked some other ponies to be Defenders of the Livewood. Scootaloo sighed.

"Wait!" somepony called. Scootaloo frowned. That sounded like...Ambermoon?

Scootaloo glanced over her shoulder. Sure enough, Lilymoon and Ambermoon were running after them.

"You escaped!" Scootaloo called with relief. She skidded to a stop, waving down Sweetie Belle and Apple Bloom. They grinned, seeing their friends approaching.

"How did you get away?" Apple Bloom

asked as Sweetie Belle blurted, "Are they chasing you, too?"

"No, everything's fine," Ambermoon said, smiling widely as she trotted closer. Scootaloo frowned. Smiling was not something that Ambermoon usually did.

"We told our family we needed to talk to you," Lilymoon explained as she approached. She was smiling, too, and there was something familiar about the way all her teeth were showing, Scootaloo thought.

"We need to talk to y'all, too!" Apple Bloom nodded. "Did you know Auntie Eclipse tried to feed us to the Timberwolves?"

The sisters' smiles didn't budge. Scootaloo frowned—what was wrong with her friends? That dreamy stare they both had made them look kinda like Blue Moon. Scootaloo's blood ran cold. Not kinda like Blue Moon. *Just* like Blue Moon.

"Uh, guys...we need to get out of here,"
Scootaloo murmured to the other Crusaders,
slowly backing away.

"What?" Sweetie Belle asked, confused.
"Why?"

It was too late. Still smiling, Ambermoon
and Lilymoon powered up their horns...and
blasted bolts of purple magic directly at
Scootaloo!

CHAPTER THREE

If she hadn't had moons of practice doing
Wonderbolts warm-ups with Rainbow Dash,
Scootaloo knew that she would've been a
goner.

But as the purple magic crackled toward
her, Scootaloo flipped backward onto her
wings. *Just like a push-up*, she could almost
hear Rainbow Dash saying, *but twenty percent
cooler.* The magic skimmed over her head,
ruffling her forelock as it passed.

With a gasp, Sweetie Belle used her magic
to lift a huge boulder, holding it like a shield
between the Crusaders and the Moon sisters
before they could attack again.

"What's happenin'?" Apple Bloom cried.

"They're under some kind of spell!"
Scootaloo blurted. "Look at their eyes!

They're like . . . zombies or something!" She winced as a still-smiling Ambermoon and Lilymoon continued to blast bolts of purple at the Crusaders. The spells bounced off Sweetie Belle's boulder, but Scootaloo could see the rock was already cracking under their assault; it wouldn't hold for long.

"Smarty-hoof! Help us!" Sweetie Belle yelled. Scootaloo heard the sound of the peryton's chiming steps approaching but didn't see the creature anywhere. Sweetie Belle glanced at the sky and whimpered.

"The sun's too bright. I don't think he has any power in the light!" she explained to her friends.

"Then we're back to my first idea," Scootaloo said. *"Run!"*

The Crusaders dashed away, just as Sweetie Belle's boulder exploded into shards of gravel. Scootaloo glanced behind her, surprised to see that Ambermoon and Lilymoon weren't chasing after them. But she did see Auntie Eclipse trotting up. The wild-haired Unicorn's eyes blazed, and Scootaloo could hear her yelling.

"Fools! You let them escape!" Auntie's shrill voice rang out. As Scootaloo gave one last look back, she saw Auntie charge up her horn and fire a spell.

Scootaloo winced as the cold touch of Auntie's magic splashed over her flank and rippled on toward her friends.

"What was that?" Apple Bloom cried.

"Auntie Eclipse just tried to hit us with a spell," Scootaloo panted as she ran. "But I don't think it worked. I don't feel any different—"

And that's when her hoof snagged on

a root. Tumbling, Scootaloo somersaulted forward to crash into Sweetie Belle and Apple Bloom, knocking them all off a cliff!

The Crusaders screamed as they fell, bouncing down the stony slope, brambles and branches ripping at their manes.

CHAPTER FOUR

Scootaloo was certain they'd hit every rock, tree, and thorn on the way down the hill. Her whole body felt so bruised, she wouldn't be surprised if it were as purple as Twilight Sparkle.

Apple Bloom tugged at a prickly bush in an attempt to rip her bow loose from where it had snagged. With a *riiiip*, the fabric gave way, sending her head over hooves.

"Whooaaa! Oof."

Sweetie Belle spit out a mouthful of leaves as she sat up, then brightened.

"Look! We made it out of the Everfree Forest!" She pointed happily. Scootaloo sighed with relief. Twilight's castle wasn't too far away. The sooner they could put their problems in the Princess of Friendship's

hooves, the better. Scootaloo was sure
Twilight would be able to reverse whatever
weird mind control Auntie had over
Ambermoon and Lilymoon. She just hoped
her friends could hang on until then.

But the three fillies hadn't taken more
than two steps when dark storm clouds drifted
across the sky.

"That's funny," Apple Bloom said. "I could
have sworn those weren't there a moment ago."

A jag of lightning ripped through the
clouds, followed by a boom of thunder that
momentarily deafened the fillies. Rain began
to pour down in sheets, drenching them.

"Of course it happens when we're out of
the Forest," Scootaloo grumbled, looking
around for trees they could take shelter under.
There wasn't so much as a shrub nearby.

"Over here!" Sweetie Belle beckoned.
Scootaloo looked to see that her friend was

heading for a rickety fruit stand on the side of the road. She dashed after the Unicorn.

A soggy Apple Bloom, Scootaloo, and Sweetie Belle ducked into the shelter. Matilda the Donkey and Mr. Cake were already inside. They greeted the Crusaders.

"Come in, come in! My goodness, I don't know where that storm came from!" Matilda said. Mr. Cake nodded, wringing out his tail with his hooves.

"Good thing this fruit stand was here," Apple Bloom agreed, patting the wall with a hoof. The weathered wood groaned under the impact. Scootaloo watched in horror as the ancient wall began to tilt.

"Uh-oh," said Mr. Cake. He leaped to brace the wooden beams before the whole stand collapsed.

"We need something to prop it up!" Matilda announced, looking around.

"Try this!" Sweetie Belle called, struggling to lift a bench at the back of the stand. Scootaloo hurried to help her. Attached to the bottom of the bench was what looked like a large melon. Except, Scootaloo noticed, it was buzzing. That was weird. Unless...

"Uh, Sweetie Belle? Maybe we shouldn't move this," Scootaloo said, gently lowering her end of the bench. Too late. The "melon" suddenly shook as hundreds of furious wasps flew out.

"Wasps' nest!" Mr. Cake yelled. He let go of the beams he was holding and raced out of the lean-to. The wall, no longer supported, began to collapse. Matilda dove to hold it up, but just then, a wasp landed on her rump.

Scootaloo winced as the angry insect stung the Donkey's sensitive hindquarters.

With a bellow of pain, Matilda bucked, her flying hooves knocking down another wall. It was too much for the ragged fruit stand. Timbers creaked in protest, and the whole thing collapsed.

The Crusaders dove out into the rain, a cloud of humming wasps hot on their tails. Matilda stomped down the road toward Ponyville. Scootaloo tried to follow, but the ground was so slick from the downpour, she slipped and fell face-first into a mud puddle. Apple Bloom and Sweetie Belle tripped over her prone form, and with a murky splash, the three Crusaders were covered in muck. The wasps, disgusted, flew away.

"At least the rain will wash us off," Sweetie Belle said. Scootaloo appreciated her friend's attempt to always see the bright side of things. Of course, it was at that moment that the storm clouds chose to part, hot sun beaming down on the mud-soaked trio. Scootaloo could already feel her coat starting to itch as the wet dirt baked into it. Walking to Twilight's castle was going to be miserable.

CHAPTER FIVE

The mud-encrusted Crusaders slowly trudged toward Ponyville. Hearing the clatter of approaching wheels, Scootaloo turned to see a familiar magic caravan trundling toward them. "It's Trixie! I bet she'll give us a ride!" she said. The Crusaders waved their hooves frantically as the wagon approached.

"Who hails the *Grrrreat* and Powerful Trixie?" the blue Unicorn asked as she trotted up. Scootaloo was surprised she didn't recognize them.

"It's us, the Cutie Mark Crusaders!" Apple Bloom said.

"Really? You look more like mud trolls." Trixie sniffed.

"Can you take us to Twilight's castle? It's *really* important," Sweetie Belle begged.

Trixie frowned. Scootaloo knew she wasn't a big fan of Twilight.

"Like, the fate of Equestria important," Scootaloo added.

"I suppose." Trixie sighed and gestured to her caravan. But as the Crusaders headed for the entrance, she held up a hoof. "*After* you scrub yourselves off. I don't want you tracking mud on my magic carpet."

"If she has a magic carpet, why does she drive a cart?" Apple Bloom grumbled to her friends.

"I think I can clean us up," Sweetie Belle said. "Rarity taught me a spell for getting stains out of silk!" Her horn glowed, and magic washed over the Crusaders.

Scootaloo immediately knew something had gone wrong. Her mane and tail felt funny. She looked at her friends to see that though they were clean, every hair on their body was standing straight out. They looked as if they'd been blown dry by the wind-force of a hundred Dizzitrons. Trixie nearly fell over laughing.

"Maybe it works better on clothes," she chortled.

The embarrassed Crusaders climbed aboard the wagon. After their long trek through the Forest and everything that had happened since, Scootaloo was grateful for a rest. She'd just gotten comfortable when the wagon hit a bump.

A box of smoke bombs jarred loose from a high shelf.

The Crusaders barely dodged in time as the box crashed to the floor, setting off every smoke bomb inside with a purple *poof*!

Scootaloo choked, blindly feeling her way through the colorful cloud toward the wagon's exit.

As the gasping Crusaders stumbled free, they found a furious Trixie staring at her wagon. One of its wheels had snapped off, probably going over that bump, Scootaloo thought.

"My wagon is broken!" Trixie moaned. "Do you know what this means?"

"We're walking to Twilight's castle?" Apple Bloom guessed.

"My show tonight will have to be canceled. You three are bad luck!" She sniffed again.

"But we didn't do anything," Scootaloo protested.

There was no reasoning with Trixie.

"Just go!" she demanded, shooing the Crusaders away with her hooves.

Scootaloo shrugged to her friends, and dejectedly, they started off down the road again.

"Do you think Trixie's right?" Sweetie Belle asked a few moments later. "Nothing's gone right for us ever since we left the Forest."

"But why would we get bad luck all of a sudden?" Apple Bloom frowned. "Nothin' happened to cause it."

Scootaloo grimaced, the slow realization dawning that in fact something *had* happened. She'd thought Auntie Eclipse's spell was a dud, but…

"Let me try something," Scootaloo said. "Anypony have a bit?"

Sweetie Belle levitated over a coin. Scootaloo held it in her hoof.

"You call manes or tails. If you're right, there's nothing wrong with our luck. But if we can't guess right no matter how many tries… then maybe something's up. Call it," she told Sweetie Belle.

"Manes!" Sweetie Belle said. The Crusaders

watched the coin as it flipped from Scootaloo's hoof and arced through the air, end over end. But before it could land, a frog hopped into its path, whipped out its tongue, and caught the bit. With a gulp, the coin was gone.

"Uh, is that manes or tails?" Apple Bloom asked.

"Neither," Scootaloo said, trying not to panic. The chances of that happening were a bazillion to one. "I think...we're cursed," she said.

CHAPTER SIX

"Cursed?" Sweetie Belle squeaked.

"It must have been Auntie Eclipse's spell! Whatever we try to do, bad things happen to us!" Scootaloo blurted.

"We have to tell Twilight about this." Apple Bloom gasped. "She'll be able to help us!"

"Even if we can get to her, I think our bad luck spills onto whoever's near us," Scootaloo said, remembering what had happened to Mr. Cake, Matilda, and Trixie. "We're not safe for *any*pony!"

A rustling in the bushes nearby startled the Crusaders. They backed up, huddling together. Now that she knew they were cursed, Scootaloo was afraid to see what would happen next. Nopony could predict what was hiding in those leaves. A basilisk? Auntie Eclipse? Queen Chrysalis, back for revenge?

The Crusaders gasped as a figure stepped from the bush.

Starlight Glimmer looked at them in surprise.

"Uh, is something wrong?" she asked.

"Stay back!" Scootaloo warned.

"We're cursed with bad luck!" Sweetie Belle cried.

Starlight raised one eyebrow as she studied them.

"You seem okay to me." She shrugged.

"Show her the bit flip," Apple Bloom said.

Sweetie Belle passed Scootaloo another coin.

"Manes or tails?" Scootaloo asked Starlight.

"Uh . . . tails," she said.

Scootaloo flipped the coin. It tumbled end over end through the air . . . and landed on her hoof, tail-side up. Scootaloo frowned. That was weird. She flipped the coin again. The same thing happened. She flipped it one more time.

"Am I supposed to be seeing something weird?" Starlight asked skeptically.

"We thought Auntie Eclipse cast a bad-luck spell on us," Scootaloo explained.

"Auntie Eclipse? Isn't she one of the ponies who just moved into the house on Horseshoe Hill?" Starlight asked.

The Crusaders nodded, explaining in a rush everything that had happened the night before and the Moon family's evil plans. Starlight blinked in surprise.

"We'd better get you to Twilight. I just

saw her in town. Come on!" Starlight trotted off down the road. Relieved to have found help, the Crusaders followed.

"Maybe all the bad luck was just a coincidence," Scootaloo told her friends hopefully. Suddenly, pounding hoofbeats shook the road. Scootaloo glanced up to see a stampede of cows headed right for the Crusaders.

"Maybe not!" yelped Sweetie Belle.

Starlight looked back to see what was happening and gaped in disbelief. She raced to the Crusaders. As soon as she drew near, the herd of cows parted around them, safely thundering past on either side.

"Okay…that was strange," Starlight admitted. She looked thoughtful. "I wonder if there's a curse on you after all. Let's see… you stay there." Starlight slowly backed away from the Crusaders. Sure enough, as soon as she was a few pony lengths away, a sinkhole opened beneath Sweetie Belle. She shrieked and started to fall. Apple Bloom, Scootaloo, and Starlight dove for her, pulling her up just before she could plummet into darkness.

"*That* was more than a coincidence," Starlight admitted. "It looks as if your bad luck stops only when I'm close by. Must be my warding spell."

"What's that?" Scootaloo asked. She didn't know much about magic. But if it was somehow keeping her safe, she was eager to learn more.

"It's just a protection bubble against dark magic I keep around myself." Starlight shrugged. "Former villain. Old habits die hard. Can't be too careful." She smiled.

"Can you put one on us?" Sweetie Belle asked hopefully. Starlight nodded.

"I think that's an excellent idea. At least

until we can find you a cure." But as she started to cast her spell, nothing happened. Starlight frowned and tapped a hoof to her horn. It glowed briefly but quickly fizzled. She sighed. "Oh...the curse on you is so powerful, it's taking all my magic to block it. As long as you're in my protection bubble, I can't do any other spells! Maybe I should just go get Twilight for you—"

"*No!*" Sweetie Belle blurted. Scootaloo couldn't blame her friend. That sinkhole had been pretty scary. If Starlight left now, who knew *what* bad things might happen to them.

"You're right—too dangerous," Starlight agreed. "We'd better stick together. But before we find Twilight, we need to get rid of your curse, just in case."

"In case what?" Scootaloo asked, dread creeping into her voice.

"I'm not sure how long my magic can protect four ponies," Starlight said, frowning, "and if you're still cursed when we get to Twilight and the others..."

Scootaloo didn't even want to think about what that would mean.

CHAPTER SEVEN

Starlight Glimmer had explained to the
Crusaders that to undo their curse, she
needed information about the magic of
the pony who'd cast it. The Crusaders
told Starlight everything they knew about
Auntie Eclipse, but they didn't have the
right details to help her unravel the bad-
luck spell. Unfortunately, the only place
Scootaloo could think of to learn more
about Auntie Eclipse was the spooky house
perched atop Horseshoe Hill. Sweetie Belle
flatly refused to go near it, but Apple Bloom
reminded her that they had overheard Auntie
Eclipse tell Lilymoon and Ambermoon they
wouldn't be returning home all day. Plus,
they didn't really have any other choice,
Scootaloo realized. Which was how the

four of them found themselves sneaking down the long, dusty hallway toward Auntie Eclipse's library.

Starlight nudged open the creaky door, and the musty smell of books and strange herbs wafted from the gloom. Scootaloo peered inside anxiously. Auntie Eclipse's words rang true—nopony seemed to be home—but Scootaloo kept her ears pricked, listening for any sounds that might mean the Moon family had returned. Not that she could hear anything over the pounding of her heart.

"We need to find something magical that belongs to Auntie Eclipse," Starlight instructed the Crusaders. "But stay close..." she warned them. "Your curse will kick in the moment you stick one hoof out of my safety bubble." The Crusaders nodded. Scootaloo searched the library shelves, collecting an armful of books and scrolls, while Apple Bloom rummaged in the drawers of a cobweb-draped desk. Sweetie Belle sniffed a vial of potion and gagged. They all made sure to stay as close to Starlight as possible.

"The only thing I'm learning about Auntie Eclipse is that she doesn't like cleaning up very much." Sweetie Belle coughed.

Scootaloo flipped through the books she'd gathered. Most were in Old Ponish, and she couldn't read them. But one slim volume was in a spidery script. It looked like some sort of journal. Scootaloo narrowed her eyes, trying to make out the words. . . .

And suddenly, the world shifted.

Scootaloo blinked. She was standing on the cobblestones of an old village, far from Ponyville. She looked around in surprise. In the town square, red-roofed houses flanked a huge fountain of a rearing Alicorn with bat wings. But how had she gotten there? Where was the library? And Starlight and Sweetie Belle and Apple Bloom?

A handsome blue Unicorn walked with a smiling Unicorn mare by the town fountain. Scootaloo ran up to them.

"Excuse me," she said breathlessly. "But what is this place?" The Unicorns didn't even look up. Instead, they walked through Scootaloo as if she wasn't even there!

Scootaloo yelped in shock and leaped back. "Ghosts!" she screamed, pointing at the Unicorns. Then her eyes fell on her hoof. It was translucent, and she could see the street cobbles beneath it. Scootaloo gasped. *"I'm a ghost!"*

As her mind tried to grasp what could possibly be going on, the male Unicorn used his horn to draw the water out of the fountain into a heart in the air. The mare laughed and nuzzled noses with him. It would be kinda cute, Scootaloo thought, if she weren't freaking out about suddenly being see-through in the middle of a strange town. Then, with a *flash*, the scene shifted.

The same two Unicorns were now inside a hospital. The male Unicorn was in bed, racked with a fit of coughing. The Unicorn mare anxiously watched over him, her hoof on his. She turned to an Earth pony doctor, but he shook his head. Bursting into tears, the female Unicorn rushed from the room. Despite the oddness of the situation, Scootaloo couldn't help but be drawn to what was happening.

Another *flash*, and now she was following the Unicorn mare to a strange cottage on the outskirts of the village. The mare pounded on the door, and it opened slowly to reveal…Auntie Eclipse! Scootaloo gasped and tried to hide behind a rock before she remembered nopony could see or hear her. Auntie looked exactly the same. With her familiar evil smile, she extended a potion to the mare. But before the mare could take it, Auntie held out a scroll and a pen. *It must be some kind of contract*, Scootaloo thought. *Maybe payment for the potion.* Auntie's eyes grew greedy as the desperate mare signed the scroll.

"Don't do it!" Scootaloo yelled to the mare, forgetting nopony could hear her.

The setting shifted again, and Scootaloo was now back in the town square. It was decorated for a wedding, with garlands of flowers draping the buildings and cheerful swaths of color hung from lamppost to lamppost.

The blue Unicorn had obviously recovered,

as he stood next to his bride. Their shared smiles were so full of love, Scootaloo almost missed seeing that Auntie Eclipse was at the wedding, too. She was also smiling, but it was a cold, cruel smile. Scootaloo shuddered as Auntie held up the contract and winked at the Unicorn mare. Whatever that piece of paper said, Scootaloo knew it wasn't good.

Time seemed to speed by in a rush, and Scootaloo was disoriented to find herself inside a cozy house. The Unicorn couple cuddled two Unicorn foals: one purple with blue-and-black-streaked hair, the other blue with purple-and-white-streaked hair. Suddenly Scootaloo realized why they were all so familiar....

"It's Lilymoon and Ambermoon," she gasped. But that would make the two older Unicorns Blue Moon and Lumi Nation.... They looked so different than when she'd last seen them. Not creepy at all. What had happened to them?

As if in answer to Scootaloo's question, the door to the house slammed open with a gust of wind. Standing in the doorway was Auntie Eclipse. Lumi Nation shook her head, and Blue Moon moved to stand in front of the small fillies. But Auntie pulled out the scroll and pointed a hoof to it. Defeated, Lumi Nation lowered her head. Grinning hideously, Auntie touched her horn to the adult Unicorns' flanks. Scootaloo leaned in to watch as a bright moon, smoke, and lightning appeared over their cutie marks.

"Auntie gave them matching marks!" she breathed. But the old sorceress wasn't finished yet. She blasted Lumi Nation and Blue Moon with a spell so bright, Scootaloo had to close her eyes. When she opened them again, Blue

Moon's gaze was vacant, and his teeth glinted in an eerie grin. Lumi Nation looked at Blue Moon sadly, tears streaming down her face. Auntie pointed, and the Unicorns stepped aside for her to lean over the foals.

"Leave my friends alone!" Scootaloo yelled, rushing over to stop the old Unicorn. But she ran straight through Auntie Eclipse. There was nothing she could do....

CHAPTER EIGHT

With a loud *thump*, Scootaloo dropped to the
floor. She blinked, surprised to find herself
back in Auntie Eclipse's dusty library. The
journal she had opened lay closed on the floor
beside her.

"What...just...happened?" Sweetie Belle
asked, her eyes huge.

"Lumi Nation made some kinda bargain
with Auntie Eclipse! She's the one who turned
'em into zombie ponies!" Apple Bloom
blurted.

"Wait. You saw that, too?" Scootaloo
asked. "How? And where were we, anyway?"

"Trotsylvania," Starlight said, looking
just as surprised as Scootaloo felt. "You found
Lumi Nation's mementorial."

"Her what?" Scootaloo frowned.

"Mementorial. It's like a magic journal. You write down memories of what happened in your life. But instead of reading it, you feel it, just as it took place," Starlight explained.

"I wonder if Auntie Eclipse has one, too," Sweetie Belle mused.

"Yeah! If we find it, maybe we'll know what her plans are to get into the Livewood! Then we'll be able to stop her!" Apple Bloom hopped up excitedly and raced toward the library shelves.

"Wait, Apple Bloom!" Scootaloo called. But it was too late. In her enthusiasm, Apple Bloom had moved out of Starlight's protective bubble. The bad-luck curse was back. With an ominous rumble, the shelves of the library quivered.

"Oops," Apple Bloom whispered. She ran

back to her friends, but the damage had been done. The library shelves were collapsing, blocking the doors and trapping them in an avalanche of books.

"You must have triggered some kind of security spell," Starlight yelled. "Everypony, under here!" She beckoned them to a sturdy reading table.

Scootaloo dove for the shelter, the other Crusaders and Starlight squeezing in beside her. The library continued to shake around them, books falling in dusty cascades. When they finally stopped, the table was completely buried.

Sweetie Belle shoved at the wall of books entombing them.

"It'll take us days to dig our way out of here," she whimpered.

"Well, start digging!" Scootaloo said,

pulling a book out of the pile. Another book instantly slid in to replace it. The entire pile rumbled dangerously.

"Maybe that's not the best idea." Apple Bloom stared at the books warily. Scootaloo kicked the floor angrily.

"We're supposed to protect the Livewood? We can't even make it out of a library!"

"Okay, everypony. Take a breath," Starlight said, looking pretty nervous herself. "Even when things seem hopeless, there're always options."

"What options? We're trapped, we're cursed, and you can't use any magic." Scootaloo groaned.

"True," said Starlight, "but when the Changelings took Twilight and the others, none of us could use magic, either. And even though it seemed impossible, we kept trying. Even Discord..." Starlight trailed off mid-sentence.

"Even Discord what?" Apple Bloom asked. Starlight chewed her lip thoughtfully.

"Could that work?" Starlight mumbled to herself. "Not while my wards are up. But if I let them down..." She glanced at the Crusaders.

Scootaloo looked at the others; it was clear none of them had any idea what Starlight was talking about.

Finally, Starlight seemed to make up her mind. "I think I know a way out of here. But I'm going to have to cast a spell," she explained. "That means I need to release the magic that's keeping us safe."

"So we'll go back to being cursed again?" Apple Bloom asked. Starlight nodded.

"And you'll be in just as much danger because you're right next to us," Sweetie Belle added, eyes wide.

"It's risky, but so is staying here," Starlight said firmly. "I need the three of you to keep perfectly still. The less you do, the less the curse has to work with. One step, a single word, *anything* can set it off. I just need a minute."

Scootaloo looked at the others. She could tell they were both as nervous as she was. She was glad Starlight was here to help them, but it also proved once again that they were *way* out of their depth.

"Okay, y'all," Apple Bloom said, "stand next to one another and don't move a muscle." The Crusaders lined up and nodded to Starlight.

"Here we go," she said. Her horn glowed briefly, and Scootaloo could see the faint shimmer of a protective bubble flash briefly before fizzling away. She didn't feel any different, but she knew they were back to being unlucky.

Starlight's horn lit up as she quickly started some kind of spell. Scootaloo focused on not moving. Above her she heard a book shift. She was afraid to even glance up to see what was happening. But she could see something out of the corner of her eye. What was that? Dust! It was dust from the table. She watched the dust slowly twirl and dance in the air in front of her.

It slipped into her nose.

She could feel it tickle the inside of her nostril.

She could feel the sneeze coming on. She tried to hold it in.

"Achoo." The slightest, smallest sneeze slipped out. It was all the curse needed.

The books above rumbled. One of the table legs splintered.

"Starlight..." Sweetie Belle whispered.

"Almost got it," Starlight said, horn glowing bright. The tabletop groaned loudly. Books poured in as if they were being pushed. Another one of the legs snapped. *"There!"* Starlight yelled.

A glowing doorway appeared, shimmering in midair. Scootaloo's jaw dropped.

"Go!" Starlight yelled, gesturing for them to step through. The Crusaders rushed toward the door. Above them, Scootaloo heard the table *crack*! Books came crashing toward them. As Scootaloo ran through the glowing doorway, she turned back to see Starlight barely make it through, just as the wave of books crashed down behind her. They would have been crushed!

With a sigh of relief, Scootaloo turned to see where Starlight had brought them. Stars shimmered. A bright comet streamed past and...a tiny rhino on roller skates sped by?

"Where are we?" Scootaloo whispered. She could barely hear Starlight's voice echoing after her.

"Discord's realm..."

CHAPTER NINE

"Discord?" Apple Bloom yelled. Three umbrellas flapped by behind her, squawking at one another loudly. Scootaloo looked down. They were standing on a fluffy marshmallow.

"We're in the realm of chaos," Starlight explained. Her horn flashed, and Scootaloo saw the protective bubble come back to life. "Stay close to me," Starlight reminded them.

"Right. The curse," Sweetie Belle muttered as she watched the three umbrellas open up to catch a breeze and soar off into the distance.

"The curse *and* the chaos," Starlight added, looking around nervously. "This is no place for ponies. If we get separated, we might never find one another again."

Scootaloo jumped as something touched her hoof. She looked down. A tiny saucer of milk nuzzled against her, purring.

"What exactly are we doing here?" she asked.

"Escaping," Starlight said as she stepped carefully along the top of the marshmallow. "Our objective is still the same: get rid of this curse and get you to Twilight. This is just a . . . detour." She hopped from the edge of their marshmallow to another one. The Crusaders looked at one another, shrugged, and followed after.

"Why didn't you just teleport us all to the castle?" Scootaloo insisted. "Wouldn't that have been easier?"

"Not with your curse." Starlight glanced back. "Teleporting four ponies across Ponyville? That could have been bad."

"How is this any better?" Scootaloo could

feel the frustration building up inside her. She hated being so helpless, and the weirdness of this place was making her feel completely lost and out of control.

Starlight paused and turned to the Crusaders. "Sorry. This is kind of a lot, isn't it?" she said sheepishly. "Okay. The realm of chaos is right next to our realm, the regular world. They're like...peanut butter and jelly!"

Scootaloo's stomach growled.

"Sorry," she said.

"Magically moving all of us from one place to another is a *big* move, with lots of ways for the curse to harm us. You saw what happened when all you did was sneeze." Scootaloo didn't need to be reminded. "So instead of risking something big, I ripped a tiny little hole between our realm and the realm of chaos, so we could slip through and get out of that library. Still dangerous, but a much smaller step." She gestured to their strange surroundings. "Now we just take a quick walk, open another small hole, and we're right back in Ponyville."

"That...actually sounds pretty simple!" Apple Bloom said, relief in her voice.

It wasn't simple.

They walked for a long time. They hopped over marshmallows, crossed rivers of chocolate milk, climbed up what seemed like a really long cat's tail...and it just kept getting weirder.

Occasionally, Starlight would make them all stand perfectly still, disable her protective spell, open a glowing door, and peek out.

One door opened in Yakyakistan.

One door opened near Mount Aris.

One door opened on the moon!

Scootaloo yawned. She had no idea how

many doors they had tried to open, all she knew was that she was tired, hungry, and hoofsore. Her friends looked just as exhausted as she was. *None* of them had slept in what felt like days.

Starlight stifled a yawn of her own. "I've got a good feeling about this one," she said as she opened yet another door. Salty water rushed through. The door must have opened at the bottom of the ocean! Scootaloo was suddenly immersed in the raging water. She choked and flailed helplessly. She tried to swim toward her friends, but the current was too strong. She felt herself getting swept away....

And suddenly found herself inside a large bubble, alongside Apple Bloom, Sweetie Belle, and Starlight!

"You know...it really is *rude* to rip a hole into somecreature's realm and sneak in without at least sending a letter first," a cultured voice said with a hint of annoyance. Scootaloo turned toward the voice.

Discord sat on the back of a turtle, sipping tea from a snail shell.

CHAPTER TEN

"Hello, Discord," Starlight said, shaking her mane dry. "Always a pleasure."

"A *pleasure*?" Discord said incredulously. "What is pleasurable about popping into my realm unannounced and causing all kinds of trouble? Annoyance is more like it."

"Well, now you know how it feels when you do it!" Starlight smirked. Discord arched an eyebrow, reached up, and poked a hole in the bubble. Water slowly poured in.

"With an attitude like that, I'm not sure why I should bother helping you," he said airily. Sweetie Belle and Apple Bloom backed away from the water, panicked.

"Discord—" Starlight began, annoyed.

"Stop messing around! You're friends with our friends. You have to help us. That's what friends *do*!" Scootaloo yelled. Discord looked down, as if seeing her for the first time.

"You're the little Rainbow Dash," he observed. "You may not fly like her, but you certainly have her attitude." He snapped his talons.

Scootaloo found herself in a comfy chair in front of a warm fire. She glanced to her left and saw Apple Bloom and Sweetie Belle wrapped in cozy blankets on a couch next to her. Starlight was curled up in front of the fire with a ball of yarn in front of her. She knocked the yarn away with her hoof and sat up.

"Discord, seriously—" she huffed. The Draconequus held up a claw, shushing her.

"Hold that thought; I want to speak with the main characters in this story." He turned to the Crusaders. "Now, why are the mini Mane Three wandering around in my backyard?"

"Starlight was tryin' to help us get to Twilight," Apple Bloom began.

"And of course, being Starlight Glimmer, she picked the most convoluted magical means of going there?" Discord asked innocently. He turned to Starlight. "Haven't you heard of a road?"

"They're cursed," Starlight huffed again. "Everything bad that can possibly happen to them *does*. Same for anypony around them. They're only safe near me because of my protective—"

"Yes, yes, yes." Discord waved his paw dismissively. He glanced at Scootaloo. "You. The little scowly one with tiny wings. You seem very emo right now. What's going on?"

Scootaloo was surprised to find her eyes

filling with tears. She felt all her stress and fear bubbling up as if it suddenly needed to get out.

"What's going on? We've been attacked by Timberwolves, our friends are pony zombies, and we have this curse on us, so we can't even get to our families and friends for help. Anypony besides Starlight who gets close to us gets hurt. And without Starlight we wouldn't even have made it this far! Princess Luna says we're supposed to be the Defenders of the Livewood, but I don't think we can do it on our own. I don't wanna let down all of Equestria!" Scootaloo took a big breath. She looked around at the others. They were all staring at her, wide-eyed.

A *ding* chimed from another room.

"*Ah!* That's my spinach puffs. I'll go get those and give you a minute to process...all that." Discord, now wearing a flowery apron, floated into the next room.

"I didn't know you felt that way," Apple Bloom said quietly.

"You're always so confident." Scootaloo sniffed. "I felt as if I'd be letting you down if I told you how worried about all this I was."

"You think I'm *not* worried?" Sweetie Belle squeaked. "I have no idea how we're supposed to protect the Livewood. I was sure Luna made a mistake!"

"I thought the same thing!" Scootaloo exclaimed. She was relieved she wasn't the only one.

"I don't think that," Apple Bloom said, looking back and forth at Scootaloo and Sweetie Belle. "But that's 'cause I got the two of you standin' next to me."

"But, Apple Bloom—" Scootaloo began. Apple Bloom shook her head.

"We got that bogle outta the Schoolhouse. Sweetie Belle faced off against Timberwolves twice. *You* stood up to your biggest fear. We've fought all kindsa crazy, and we're still standin'. So if Princess Luna says we got what it takes, I believe her."

Scootaloo leaped onto the couch between her two best friends, grabbed them with her hooves, and squeezed tight.

"You guys are the best friends a pony could ever ask for." Scootaloo smiled. She still had no idea what they were going to do. But she would follow these two fillies anywhere.

"Ahem." The three fillies turned to see Starlight smiling at them.

"Oh. Hey, Starlight. We kinda forgot you were there," Apple Bloom said, grinning.

"I noticed." Starlight smiled. She turned to Scootaloo. "I was only trying to protect you back there. But you three are pretty resourceful. I have no doubt that with or without me, you would have eventually

broken Auntie Eclipse's curse on your own."
A loud clatter caught their attention. They
turned to see Discord, his spinach puffs
scattered on the floor.

"Auntie Eclipse? Now, *there's* a name I
haven't heard in a while."

CHAPTER ELEVEN

"You know her?" Sweetie Belle asked.

"Frizzy mane? Laugh like a cragadile? Oh, we are well acquainted. She actually thought she could capture me and force me to do her bidding. Spoiler alert: She didn't. But that shriveled-up excuse for a pony has been messing with magic since before I was turned into stone!"

Scootaloo's mouth dropped open.

"But . . . you were turned to stone by Celestia and Luna thousands of moons ago," Apple Bloom pointed out.

"How old *is* she?" Scootaloo asked.

"How should I know? I wasn't very nice back then. Didn't get invited to birthday parties." Discord snapped his claws, and the spinach puffs grew legs and marched back onto the tray. He picked it up and offered it to Sweetie Belle.

"No, thanks." She shuddered.

"If that's true, then Auntie Eclipse really is as dangerous as the three of you said she was." Starlight looked meaningfully at Discord. "All the *more* reason to get back to Twilight *quickly*?"

"*Oh*, I see!" Discord drawled dramatically. "You expect me to point you in the proper direction out of here."

"It would be the *friendly* thing to do," Starlight said through gritted teeth.

"*Mmm-hmm.* And we're no longer worried about the curse a centuries-old witch put on the three of them?" Discord motioned to the Crusaders. "I'm sure sending three cursed fillies to the six most powerful ponies in Equestria couldn't go wrong. *At. All.*"

"Maybe you could go tell our sisters and the others what's goin' on?" Apple Bloom asked Discord hopefully.

"That's...I can't believe I didn't think of that!" Starlight said, surprised.

"It didn't involve you showing off all those fancy powers of yours, so why would you?" Discord smiled innocently. He turned to Apple Bloom. "I, of course, *could* go tell them everything." His eyes briefly darted to Scootaloo. "But then you would have even *more* ponies rushing to your rescue. And as a...*friend*...I wouldn't want to get in the way of a young filly's personal growth."

"What does that mean?" Scootaloo asked.

"It means he's not being helpful," Starlight said, glaring at him.

"You mean the way *you're* helping by being so overprotective about this curse?" Discord snapped his talons. The room stretched out, separating Starlight from the Crusaders.

"*No!*" Starlight yelled.

"The curse!" Sweetie Belle screamed.

"Hold on, y'all!" Apple Bloom closed her eyes tight, waiting for something bad to happen. Scootaloo couldn't believe Discord would put them in danger like that. She knew he was annoying, but he was supposed to be a good guy now!

Scootaloo looked around. Nothing was happening. They seemed fine. She waved a hoof in the air. No wasps, no rain. No storm clouds.

"You guys"—Scootaloo trotted around in a circle, making sure—"I think...I think the curse is gone?" The others watched her warily. Then they also started waving their hooves. Soon they were all running around, leaping and cheering. There was no more curse!

Starlight came rushing over to them from across the now very *long* room.

"Are you all okay?" she called.

"The curse is gone!" Scootaloo called back.

"Actually . . . no." Discord sat nearby, wearing 3-D glasses and eating popcorn. "Bad-luck curses work using logic. They figure out the worst possible thing that *could* happen and make it come true. But there's no logic here. It's all chaos!" Several toads wearing turbans danced by in the background. "With no logic, there's no luck. So there's nothing for the spell to work with. You've been safe here the entire time!"

"Seriously?" Starlight was fuming. "If I had known they were all safe, I could have left them here and gotten Twilight myself! Why are you just telling us this *now*?"

Discord lowered his glasses and grinned at her. "Because this isn't a *Starlight Glimmer saves the day* story. *This* is a *Cutie Mark Crusaders put the clues together and solve the mystery* story. Obviously." He turned to the Crusaders. "So?"

"The curse is gonna be back as soon as we leave your realm and go to Ponyville?" Apple Bloom asked. A bell dinged above her head.

"Correct!" Discord, now dressed as a game-show host, announced.

"And anything we try to do is gonna backfire on us?" Sweetie Belle groaned. A bell dinged above her head.

"Correct!" Discord said into a microphone.

"Then there's no way to beat Auntie Eclipse and break the spell!" Scootaloo spat in annoyance. A red *X* buzzed above her head.

"Oooooh. Sorry, wrong answer." Discord frowned.

"You're being ridiculous," Starlight yelled from a set of bleachers.

"Can the studio audience *please* keep it down?" Discord shouted back. Scootaloo ground her teeth. She could see how Starlight and the others got so annoyed with Discord. He was joking around while Lilymoon and Ambermoon were in real danger! And it wasn't as if they could go ask some other pony for any help. Starlight and Discord were literally the *only* two the Crusaders could turn to. *Anypony* else they got *close* to would be just as unlucky as they—

Scootaloo threw her hoof into the air like she did when she knew the answer in Miss Cheerilee's class.

"I know how to break the curse!" she yelled.

CHAPTER TWELVE

"Are you three sure about this?" Starlight asked for the eleventh time. "It just seems... really risky." They were sitting in the back of a strange pink wagon that Discord kept calling a "dream car," whatever that was. Discord was in the front seat, driving.

"We're sure," Apple Bloom assured her. She put her hoof around Scootaloo. "If Scootaloo thinks it's gonna work, then I know we're gonna be good."

"And besides," Sweetie Belle added, "it's not as if this plan is crazier than any of the other ones we've come up with lately."

Scootaloo nodded. She was nervous, but also—for the first time since Luna had appeared in their dream—feeling sure of herself. With the other Crusaders at her side, and an idea of what exactly needed to be done, she felt ready for anything.

Discord drove the pink wagon into the yawning jaws of a massive Dragon.

Well, Scootaloo amended, *almost anything.*

"This is the most direct route to the Everfree Forest, huh?" Starlight frowned at Discord.

"No. I'm avoiding traffic," the Draconequus huffed. "But have it your way." With a snap of his talons, the entire pink wagon vanished and reappeared in the middle of a crowd of slowly moving cockatrices. Scootaloo clapped her hooves over her eyes as Starlight shouted a warning.

"Don't look at them! Their stares can turn you to stone! *Discord!*" Starlight sounded really upset.

Another talon snap, and Scootaloo peeked out to see that the wagon was now rolling through the Everfree Forest.

Discord smirked at the fuming Starlight. "Nopony likes a backseat driver, Starlight. Honestly, when are you going to realize that this isn't your narrative to control? Wait until you're *asked* for help, or you'll ruin everything these little heroes have planned."

"Is it safe to look yet?" Sweetie Belle whispered.

"That depends on yer idea of safe," Apple Bloom whispered back. "Look!"

She pointed. Through the trees ahead, Scootaloo spotted Auntie Eclipse and the rest of the Moon family. They were too far away to hear, but she could see they were standing by a familiar barrier of twisting vines. Scootaloo knew what that meant.

"She's trying to break into the Livewood again," Scootaloo breathed.

"Then we have to stop her—" Starlight blurted, and caught herself. "I mean...good luck, you three. I'm here if you need me."

Discord nodded approvingly. "Better." He brought the wagon to a stop. As everypony climbed out, he reached down and folded the whole vehicle into a small square before slipping it into a pocket. "Need to keep it safe. Convention exclusive, you know." He winked at Scootaloo. She had no idea what he was talking about.

"Thanks for your help, Discord," she said.

"Don't mention it," he replied with a wave of a claw, then added, "Seriously, don't. If creatures start thinking I'm 'nice,' they won't leave me alone. And then I'll *never* finish writing my rock opera." He waved his hands like a conductor, and several boulders nearby grew mouths that belted a high note.

And with that, he disappeared. The curse was back, and the Crusaders and Starlight were on their own.

CHAPTER THIRTEEN

"Stay close," Starlight reminded the others as they crept through the underbrush toward Auntie Eclipse. She didn't need to tell them twice, Scootaloo thought. The Crusaders were practically pressed to Starlight's flank, huddling in her protective bubble. This was definitely not the time to tempt bad luck.

Quietly, the four ponies sidled up as close as they could to the clearing around the Livewood. Blue Moon stood on top of one of the three gnarled pillars of earth and rock that faced the barrier of serpentine vines. Ambermoon was just climbing up the stairs that surrounded the second pillar, and Lumi Nation was steering Lilymoon toward the third. Behind them, Auntie Eclipse chanted a spell, her horn glowing with bloodred magic. Apple Bloom gave a soft gasp.

"They're using their matching cutie marks to open the Livewood," she hissed.

"Not if we can help it," Scootaloo murmured with determination. She looked at Sweetie Belle and Apple Bloom. They nodded. It was time.

"Watch our backs, Starlight. We'll tell you if we need help," Scootaloo said. She could see that Starlight was struggling not to give them advice, but finally, the purple Unicorn nodded, too.

"Got it. Whenever you're ready," she said. Scootaloo began their special count of three.

"Cutie…"

"Mark…" Sweetie Belle chimed in.

"Crusaders!" Apple Bloom finished. Then the trio of fillies burst into the clearing with Starlight at their heels.

Lumi Nation snapped her head around to see what was going on. Without her guidance, Lilymoon froze on her way to the pillar. Scootaloo could see that the filly's eyes were vacant and staring. She was still under some kind of zombie spell.

"Stop them!" Auntie Eclipse snarled. "Nothing can interfere with my spell!"

Wanna bet? Scootaloo thought. And with that, the Cutie Mark Crusaders turned from the pillars and charged straight at Auntie Eclipse.

Scootaloo could feel the change in the air as the three of them left Starlight's bubble of safety. The curse didn't waste any time getting to work. Apple Bloom stepped on a banana peel that Scootaloo could swear hadn't been there a moment ago. The Earth pony lost her footing and slid sideways into Sweetie Belle, who bounced into Scootaloo.

The ponies' momentum sent them sprawling forward to land in a heap.

Right at Auntie Eclipse's hooves.

Auntie leered down at the Crusaders.

Behind them, Starlight had her hooves full, fending off Lumi Nation's magical attacks. Ambermoon and Lilymoon stared into space, faint smiles on their empty-eyed faces. Blue Moon grinned maniacally atop his pillar. Nopony would come to their aid now. The Crusaders were on their own. Scootaloo gulped. If this was the end, at least she had her friends by her side.

CHAPTER FOURTEEN

"Enough of these filly games," Auntie Eclipse said mockingly. "It's time I finished you three troublemakers once and for all." Her eyes gleamed as she lowered her horn toward the Crusaders. It spit red sparks, wreathed in dark magic. Scootaloo winced.

And an overripe melon fell from the vines above to *splat* down on Auntie's head.

Auntie staggered. Yellow juice ran down her mane and into her eyes. If she hadn't been so scared, Scootaloo would've burst out laughing. The sticky melon clung to Auntie's head like a mushy helmet. Furious, the evil Unicorn tossed her head, splattering the Crusaders with flying melon pulp.

She aimed her horn at the Crusaders

again. And with a cry of rage, she let loose a powerful red blast of magic.

But the rind of the melon around her horn interfered with the spell. Instead of hitting Scootaloo and her friends, Auntie's bolt of power ricocheted at an angle...

And struck Blue Moon! With a groan, the Unicorn fell to his knees atop the pillar.

Auntie gaped. Then her eyes narrowed as she looked at the Crusaders.

"Very clever. You discovered your curse affects ponies near you. But all I have to do is walk away...." Auntie smirked. She tried to raise a hoof to take a step...and couldn't. Instead, with a squelching sound, she began to slowly sink into the ground.

Scootaloo had never been happier to be stuck in quicksand. When the ground around the trio had turned marshy, she knew their bad luck had kicked in again. Fortunately, Auntie was just as vulnerable as they were.

With a furious scream, Auntie charged up her horn again. A blast of power rippled from it, knocking over the Crusaders like a chilly wind. The ground suddenly firmed up beneath them, and the melon dropped free of Auntie's horn.

The curse was gone! Scootaloo's plan had worked!

Except that meant that Auntie was no longer cursed, either.

"Starlight! Help!" Apple Bloom, Sweetie Belle, and Scootaloo shrieked in unison.

Ducking past Lumi Nation's attack, Starlight turned her horn toward the Crusaders, hurling up a shield spell to protect them. The Crusaders shrank back as Auntie leveled a blast of red magic at them. It bounced off the shield, nearly hitting Auntie. She ground her teeth in frustration.

"Run!" Starlight called as Auntie turned her attack toward the purple Unicorn.

The trio charged for the safety of the trees . . . but suddenly magic froze them in place. Scootaloo looked out of the corner of her eye to see that Lumi Nation held them with her horn.

"You're not going anywhere," she snarled. A blur of blue crashed into Lumi, sending her tumbling and breaking her spell.

Scootaloo blinked to see Blue Moon standing over them. His eyes were clear, and his strange smile was gone. He looked like the Unicorn Scootaloo had seen in her vision from the mementorial, but older and more careworn.

"Everypony, down!" Starlight bellowed. The Crusaders and Blue Moon dropped and

flattened themselves to the ground as a huge burst of Auntie's power rolled through the clearing. The heat of the spell sizzled over Scootaloo's head. It singed the leaves and left scorch marks on the pillars. Auntie wasn't messing around anymore. That was Princess Celestia–level magic.

Starlight *poof*ed into place beside the Crusaders.

"Time to go!" she said urgently.

"Take Blue Moon, too!" Scootaloo blurted.

Starlight looked ready to argue, but she seemed to remember her conversation with Discord. Shrugging, she put one hoof on his shoulder and one on Scootaloo's. Sweetie Belle and Apple Bloom grabbed Scootaloo's wings, and with a powerful *bampf* they all teleported out of the Everfree Forest.

CHAPTER FIFTEEN

"It's weird to see him look so serious," Scootaloo whispered, eyeing Blue Moon as Twilight led him to the front of the throne room.

"But way less creepy," Sweetie Belle murmured back.

"That curse finally did somethin' right," Apple Bloom said softly. "When Auntie's magic hit him, it musta broken the zombie spell she put on him."

"Guess it turned out to be some good luck after all." Sweetie Belle smiled.

"Tell that to Matilda," Apple Bloom said.

Applejack cleared her throat and looked pointedly at the Crusaders. They quieted down as Starlight and the rest of the Mane Six took their places.

"We've heard your story from the Cutie Mark Crusaders, Blue Moon. But we still have some questions," Twilight began. "Is Auntie Eclipse really trying to open the Livewood? And is it true she forced your family into helping her?"

Blue Moon nodded sadly. Scootaloo could almost feel sorry for him. Almost.

"Auntie Eclipse has had no other goal since I met her. She believes she will take the helm of Nightmare Moon and lead Equestria into an age of darkness. She could have used any family," he said bitterly. "But when I grew sick, she tricked Lumi into pledging our loyalty to her in exchange for curing me. Now I wonder if Auntie made me sick to begin with, just so she could force Lumi to do what she wanted."

"*Waiiit*. So you *weren't* both under some kind of zombie spell to serve her? You did it willingly?" Rainbow Dash asked, flying to get into Blue Moon's face.

Blue Moon didn't flinch. Scootaloo was impressed. It took a lot of courage to stand up to Rainbow Dash when she was in cross-examination mode!

"I usually was. But not always," he admitted. "When Auntie Eclipse wanted Lumi to behave a certain way, she would put me back under her spell until Lumi completed whatever Auntie demanded. It was as if I were wearing a mask and not in control of what I was doing. Just riding along, like this…"

Blue Moon's face slipped into his terrifying grin, and Scootaloo shuddered. *That* she remembered.

"Why not just keep y'all under her spell the whole time?" Applejack wondered.

"A compulsion spell takes lots of magic."

Twilight frowned. "Holding power over even one pony for that long is a challenge."

"But controlling one pony in order to make another pony do your bidding is clever. Half the magic, twice the result," Starlight reasoned. The others glared at her. She rolled her eyes. "Oh, come on! I'm not saying it's a *good* idea. Just effective."

"And now she has the fillies under her spell?" Twilight sighed heavily. "Auntie must be more powerful than we thought."

"She didn't try anything on our girls until yesterday," Blue Moon admitted. "Auntie has been very careful, plotting each step. But now she's using as much magic as it takes, because she knows you all are onto her. And these three brave fillies," he added, nodding to Scootaloo, Sweetie Belle, and Apple Bloom, "are the only ones who have stopped her plan so far."

All eyes in the room turned to the Crusaders. Sweetie Belle blushed, Apple Bloom stood proudly, and Scootaloo just hoped this meant they wouldn't be in trouble for sneaking into the Livewood.

"Poor Ambermoon and Lilymoon," Fluttershy said. Scootaloo could see she was feeling bad about not having trusted the two fillies. "How could you let that horrible Unicorn turn them into zombies?" She frowned at Blue Moon.

"Lumi Nation and I have tried to protect our daughters," Blue Moon said, looking down in shame. "Lumi is the strongest of all of us. Auntie always had a hard time controlling her. But the contract that binds the two of them will *give* Auntie our daughters if Lumi doesn't serve her. We are truly caught in that witch's web."

"At least you're free now," Pinkie Pie said,

trying to find a bright side. "That's gotta mess up her plans!"

But Blue Moon shook his head. "Auntie Eclipse gave *four* of us matching cutie marks. She needs only three ponies to open the Livewood. She liked having a spare. She's a planner."

Silence fell over the room as the gathered ponies realized what this meant.

"Then we have to stop her, right now!" Twilight said, stomping a hoof in determination.

"No," Starlight said.

Everypony turned to her in surprise, even Scootaloo.

"*We* don't have to stop her. *They* do." Starlight nodded to the Cutie Mark Crusaders.

"Darling, what are you saying? Of course they're brave, and they've done so much already," Rarity said, moving to put a protective hoof around Sweetie Belle's shoulders. "But one doesn't send fillies against an ancient sorceress!"

"Princess Luna chose them to be Defenders of the Livewood. We can help them...but this is their story," Starlight said.

Scootaloo might have been imagining it, but she thought she heard Discord sighing in relief: *"She can be taught!"*

"How do you feel about this?" Twilight asked the Crusaders. They shifted from hoof to hoof, and finally Apple Bloom spoke up.

"We know it won't be easy."

"And we're scared," Sweetie Belle added.

"But together, we're stronger than anypony," Scootaloo said. Twilight smiled, looking proudly at the three fillies.

"I know you are," Twilight said. Then she turned to the assembled ponies. "We don't

have a lot of time. I'm sure Auntie Eclipse
is attempting to open the Livewood as we
speak." She turned to look at the Cutie Mark
Crusaders. "Let's do what we can to get you
three ready to save Equestria."

Scootaloo glanced at her friends. Apple
Bloom swelled with pride. Sweetie Belle
looked mildly nauseous. Scootaloo wasn't
sure what was going to happen. But she was
ready. She knew they could do this. Right
now, she felt as if they could do anything.
The moment was only slightly ruined by
Applejack leaning down to whisper...

"But *after* you save Equestria...y'all are
still grounded."

EPILOGUE

Lumi Nation watched helplessly as Auntie Eclipse directed her daughters slowly up the pillars. She was furious with herself for doing nothing, but she knew how powerful Auntie was, and she was well aware that standing up to her wouldn't accomplish anything. She had tried. Many, many times. Lilymoon took her place atop the first pillar, staring ahead with the familiar grin Lumi had come to know so well. Moments later, Ambermoon reached the top of the second pillar, wearing the same blank expression. Auntie Eclipse turned to Lumi, her horn glowing a sickly bloodred.

"At least I don't have to waste any of my power on you, do I, dearie? You know what happens to your little brats if you try to stop me."

Lumi sighed. She did know. At least her beloved husband had escaped. Maybe once this was over and Auntie got what she wanted, she would let them all go? It was the only chance Lumi could see of getting her life back.

"Until now," Lumi whispered to herself as she slowly walked up the twisting steps of the third pillar.

"What was that?" Auntie snapped.

"Nothing," Lumi called down to her. But that wasn't true. For the first time in forever, Lumi saw the narrowest chance to escape this nightmare without putting all of Equestria at risk. Lily and Amber's friends, the Cutie Mark Crusaders. They had succeeded in thwarting Auntie where so many ponies had failed. Lumi felt something fluttering in her chest she hadn't felt in years.

Hope.

She took a final step and stared out at

the Livewood atop the third pillar. Lily's
and Amber's cutie marks glowed brightly.
A burning pain in Lumi's flank caused her
to suck in a deep breath as her cutie mark
glowed along with theirs. Ever so slowly,
the twisting vines of the Livewood began to
untangle and pull away from one another.

Beyond them, in the shadows, bells chimed
sadly.

The Livewood was open.

ENJOY MORE PONY ADVENTURES WITH THESE DVDS!